P9-CRG-761

Birthday Zoo

WRITTEN BY

Deborah Lee Rose

ILLUSTRATIONS BY

Lynn Munsinger

SCHOLASTIC INC.

New York Toronto London Auckland Sydney
Mexico City New Delhi Hong Kong Buenos Aires

To my sister, Barb, for her birthday — D. L. R.

For Brian — L. M.

No part of this publication may be reproduced in whole or in part,
or stored in a retrieval system, or transmitted in any form or by any means,
electronic, mechanical, photocopying, recording, or otherwise, without written permission of the publisher.
For information regarding permission, write to Albert Whitman & Company,
6340 Oakton Street, Morton Grove, IL 60053-2723.

ISBN 0-439-56055-1

Text copyright © 2002 by Deborah Lee Rose. Illustrations copyright © 2002 by Lynn Munsinger.
All rights reserved. Published by Scholastic Inc., 557 Broadway, New York, NY 10012,
by arrangement with Albert Whitman & Company.
SCHOLASTIC and associated logos are trademarks and/or registered trademarks of Scholastic Inc.

12 11 10 9 8 7 6 5 4   3 4 5 6 7 8/0

Printed in the U.S.A.   24

First Scholastic printing, September 2003

The paintings are rendered in pen and ink and watercolor, on Windsor Newton paper.

Design by Scott Piehl.

"Hey, what's the big deal?"
noticed the seal.

"Birthday today!"
reported the ray.

"Who is it for?"
inquired the boar.

"Kid with the presents,"
answered the pheasants.

"What do we do?"
asked the emu.

"Make everyone happy,"
said the okapi.

"But where to begin?"
asked the shy tamarin.

"Blow up balloons,"
puffed the raccoons.

"Spread out a cloth,"
directed the sloth.

"Pass out the hats,"
instructed the bats.

"Pour all the drinks,"
gurgled the lynx.

"Get them to laugh,"
advised the giraffe.

"Pin the tail on the donkey?"
suggested a monkey.

"Musical chairs!"
pleaded the bears.

"Open the gifts!"
insisted the swifts.

"Recycle the paper,"
reminded the tapir.

"Who's ready for cake?"
invited the snake.

"It's chocolate chip,"
the wolf licked her lip.

"We need some more forks!"
flurried the storks.

"Candles look loose,"
worried the moose.

"Go on, make a wish,"
burbled the fish.

"Blow hard as a whale!"
encouraged the snail.

"Your wish will come true,"
applauded the gnu.

"Happy birthday to you!"
chimed in the whole zoo.